THE HUGGABLE HOGLET

Written and illustrated by Thelma S Thacker

The Huggable Hoglet
© *Thelma S Thacker 2021*

ISBN: 978-1-922644-57-2 (Paperback)
        978-1-922644-58-9 (eBook)

 A catalogue record for this book is available from the National Library of Australia

Editor: Chloe Cran
Cover Design: Ocean Reeve Publishing
Design and Typeset: Ocean Reeve Publishing
Printed in Australia by Ocean Reeve Publishing and Clark & Mackay Printers

Published by Thelma S Thacker and Ocean Reeve Publishing
www.oceanreevepublishing.com

THE HUGGABLE HOGLET

thelma
2021

INTRODUCTION

This book reflects a year like no other. 2020 began on a positive note; in January, I had just celebrated my sixtieth birthday and had lots planned for later in the year. Then the virus happened, and the world completely changed. We were soon in lockdown, and I found myself deep in thought. A feeling of isolation was taking over. Initially, the garden, cupboards, and drawers benefited from the sudden hours and days that I found needed to be filled. Not much of an improvement happened throughout the year, and then, facing a second lockdown, I decided that, as winter approached, I needed a new project.

A 'light bulb' moment occurred, and I decided to fulfil a lifelong ambition to write and illustrate a book.

The subjects used reflected on the impact and relevance of these unprecedented times. My thoughts have been focussed on all the young people, how they were dealing with the changes, and how they would interpret these times in years to come.

Please enjoy my imaginary world, and I hope it enables others to find solace in their forced time bubble and try to use it to their advantage. I am hopeful that our youngsters are resilient and will bounce back unscathed when we can resume some sort of normality.

In loving memory of so many that lost the fight.

'Hello, world!' squealed Henrietta the hoglet as she emerged from the safety of her plant pot bed. It was a bright, fine, and sunny spring morning, and the little baby hedgehog—known as a hoglet—had been hibernating fast asleep for the past five months.

The little hoglet was dressed in her pink and purple onesie. Her little brown eyes started to sparkle as, looking around her, she spotted her friend, Harry, who was still half-asleep.

'What's been happening, Harry?' she asked. She was ready to go off and explore, but she needed a reassuring hug and a squeeze to confirm that everything was okay …

Harry had his blue pyjamas on and was listening to his favourite slumber music through his headphones. He smiled, and as he snuggled back into his bed, he said with a big yawn, 'Sorry, no hugs from me, Henrietta. You shouldn't be out in the daytime. Go back to bed and sleep well.'

Henrietta was disappointed. All she needed was a hug and some guidance after having slept so long. She couldn't understand why Harry wouldn't help her …

Henrietta stretches,
Gives a wiggle, a shake, and a shrug,
And sets off on her journey,
Searching for a hug!

Down the garden path, she skipped through the twigs and leaves. Henrietta ducked and squeezed beneath the wooden fence and continued across a lawn. It was a long way for those little legs and tiny feet! She crawled under a wire fence and then crossed a road—carefully looking both ways—before climbing up and over the kerb.

Henrietta saw a sign with an arrow pointing towards the zoo. *Surely there must be someone huggable here*, she thought. She walked quickly through the gates and along a narrow path.

There was a rustle and a snapping of twigs that rained down leaves from above. Henrietta looked up and spotted a purple and pink scarf that was wrapped loosely around a very long neck. Up and up, her eyes followed the neck—it seemed to disappear into the clouds! It was Gina the Giraffe, who was busy eating her lunch and collecting leaves in her basket to take home for her friends.

'Sorry to interrupt your lunch, Gina!' shouted Henrietta. 'But, please, may I have a hug?'

'Not at the moment,' Gina replied. 'I'm way too tall for hugs!' She fluttered her long eye-lashes and carried on munching away …

Henrietta stretches,
Gives a wiggle, a shake, and a shrug,
And sets off on her journey,
Searching for a hug!

Henrietta continued past the trees and crossed a dusty pathway. She then spied a deep pool of water. It looked like it was playtime for Henry the Hippo. She heard laughter and saw dirty water splashing everywhere. She glimpsed a pair of bright red shorts and the biggest hands, feet, and head appearing and disappearing in and out of the pool. *Perhaps Henry is huggable,* she thought.

'Henry, can you spare a hug?' shouted Henrietta loudly, over all the noise!

Henry bounced a ball out of the water with his head and replied, 'I'm much too muddy and wet to give hugs!' He laughed loudly as he quickly disappeared back beneath the water with a great big splash!

Henrietta stretches,
Gives a wiggle, a shake, and a shrug,
And sets off on her journey,
Searching for a hug!

Oh, well. Henrietta chuckled to herself. *At least I stayed dry!*

At that moment, something bright caught her eye as it flashed in the sunshine. Over the high fence and high up in a tree, she saw Lionel the Lion! Lionel looked splendid, lying lazily with his legs astride a large branch. He was wearing his colourful purple and green shirt and looked smart in his best brown trousers. His teeth looked big and sharp, and his eyes glistened as he smiled down at Henrietta. He looked very casual. His sunglasses were in his hand, and his golden crown was tilted and perched upon the front of his head. Henrietta should have been frightened, but she felt safe—Lionel had eaten his lunch and already had a very full tummy.

'Any friendly hugs for me today, King Lionel?' enquired Henrietta.

'I'm much too busy looking out for all the animals in my kingdom!' roared Lionel, gently swishing his tail back and forth …

Henrietta stretches,
Gives a wiggle, a shake, and a shrug,
And sets off on her journey,
Searching for a hug!

Henrietta headed out towards the bushes and rocky area. She was intrigued by the meerkat that stood tall and proud, dressed in his bright blue dungarees. His whiskers twitched, and his long tail curled upwards as it moved side-to-side with anticipation. Henrietta recognised that it was Morris, one of Harry's friends! He was popping up and down with his binoculars and getting the best views, balancing carefully whilst doing so. Morris was playing hide-and-seek!

'It's me, Henrietta,' she explained. 'Any chance of a hug?'

'I'm much too busy being nosey!' shouted Morris. With that, he quickly popped out of sight again to continue with his game …

Henrietta stretches,
Gives a wiggle, a shake, and a shrug,
And sets off on her journey,
Searching for a hug!

I'm not doing very well getting hugs, thought Henrietta. *I will try one more time and then head homeward.*

Her little legs were getting tired, so when she spotted the reptile house, she chose to look inside. *Maybe someone indoors would be a better option*, she thought to herself.

The door was slightly open, so she tiptoed inside. It was extremely warm and very peaceful.

Henrietta was startled by a hiss that got louder and louder. She looked into the snake pit. Her eyes were wide open when she realised that Sssara the Snake was looking at her from behind a pale blue mask. Her scaly skin and big, long body entwined around a large branch, moving slowly.

Henrietta was mesmerised but a little scared. 'I need a hug,' she whispered.

'Henrietta, I'm much too big and ssstrong and my sssqueezes are way too tight. Plus, my tongue is sssharp, ssso I need to wear a mask,' Sssara hissed. Her face was brown and orange with all the effort and constant hissing. 'I'm not ideal for handing out hugsss!' she said.

Henrietta quickly turned around and closed the door on her way out ...

Henrietta stretches,
Gives a wiggle, a shake, and a shrug,
And sets off on her journey,
Searching for a hug!

Henrietta walked back out the zoo gates and crossed the road carefully before heading for home. She decided to take a shortcut across the park because her little legs were aching and she needed a rest. As she walked past the play area, she could see some children playing. She heard their names being called by their mum and noticed that Edie was playing with her baby doll. She seemed to be having a lot of fun climbing the steps and then whizzing down the slide.

Nearby, Luka was practising his football skills by enthusiastically kicking and chasing his ball. Both children had their shorts and T-shirts on. They stood out in their pink and red shirts and their purple and burgundy shorts. They were soaking up the fresh air and enjoying the warm sunshine.

'Yoo-hoo!' squealed Henrietta excitedly. 'Anyone for a hug?'

The two children stopped in their tracks, saw Henrietta, and both ran towards their mum, who was standing nearby. 'We have to walk away from strangers!' Luka shouted as they both grabbed their mum's hands, and they all walked away …

Henrietta stretches,
Gives a wiggle, a shake, and a shrug,
And sets off on her journey,
Searching for a hug!

It had been a good walk around the grassy park, but by then Henrietta's whole body was aching from tiredness. She started to think about her cosy bed. Henrietta strolled along a small path and then alongside a cobbled wall towards the fence. She quickened her steps when she realised that she was nearly home. She then stumbled upon two big, furry feet and looked up. She saw Frankie the Fox with his bottom perched on the wall.

His big, bushy, brown tail, upright ears, and pointed nose blocked out the sunlight. He looked trendy in his blue jeans and a blue chequered shirt. His guitar was propped up against the wall beside him. He slyly winked at Henrietta and carried on chatting away on his telephone.

Henrietta didn't stop, but she heard Frankie say, 'I'm arranging to meet up with friends to play some music, sing, dance, and have some fun. You are welcome to come along, Henrietta. We can all share a group hug!'

'No, Frankie, I'm fine,' said Henrietta, 'I need to get home. My mum will be looking for me and wondering where I am!' Henrietta headed quickly through a small hole beneath the fence.

Henrietta stretches,
Gives a wiggle, a shake, and a shrug,
And sets off on her journey,
Searching for a hug!

As she popped up the other side of the fence, all Henrietta could hear was the sound of Harry snoring. He was still fast asleep in his leafy plant pot bed.

She was relieved to see her mum busy in the kitchen in her lovely bright green apron, preparing the beetles, caterpillars, and earthworms for their tea. 'Oh, there you are,' said Henrietta's mum. 'Are you okay, Henrietta? Where have you been?'

Henrietta replied, 'I'm feeling happy and sad, Mum. I've enjoyed my walk out, seen lots of old friends, and made some new ones.'

Henrietta told her mum all about her adventures and how none of her friends would hug her. She asked her mum, 'Why would nobody give me a hug? Not even a little squeeze. Is it because I'm too spikey?'

'Henrietta, it's not because you are spikey. Everyone has done the right thing. Whilst we were hibernating, a nasty germ has been spreading around everywhere, and it makes people feel very poorly. There have been lots of ways to avoid it and new advice on how to keep everyone safe. One thing we know is that close contact passes the bug around easily. It's very contagious. This is why nobody is huggable at the moment.' Henrietta's mum went on to explain why everyone had refused a hug.

'Harry was correct. We hedgehogs are nocturnal and usually sleep all day and venture out at night. He also suggested that we should only do one lot of exercise a day and that we need to try and limit the number of people we meet to prevent spreading the germs.

'Gina the Giraffe was trying to explain that we should try to eat healthily and keep ourselves strong enough to fight off any bugs in case we are unlucky and catch anything.

'Henry the Hippo's message was to keep our hands clean and to wash them regularly for at least thirty seconds to stop the spread of any germs before and after we touch things.

'Lionel the Lion was looking after all his kingdom's mental health and wellbeing. He was keeping his eyes on people to check they were not feeling isolated and letting everyone know he was there to support them where needed.

'Morris the Meerkat was popping in and out to see if any of his friends and family needed any shopping or help with picking things up, such as prescriptions.

'Sssara the Snake was wearing a mask to protect herself and others from catching or spreading any germs.

'Luka and Edie were keeping within their family bubbles and staying two metres away from everyone else to prevent spreading germs.

'Frankie the Fox was doing a good thing by phoning his friends and keeping in touch. People have been isolated and lonely, so this is very thoughtful, although he would be breaking the rules by inviting you to a party. It's good that you didn't go with him and you chose to come home. Social gatherings and being in small, confined spaces aren't recommended and can help spread germs.

'So, you see, Henrietta, each of them was looking out for you and each other by following the rules to help keep us all safe. If we all do a little bit to help, things will soon improve!'

Henrietta's mum then gave her the biggest hug and squeeze that any little hoglet could ever dream of. 'Most of all, our family are only allowed to hug each other for now,' said Henrietta's mum. 'So remember, hands, face, and space. Then one day, when this bad germ has gone, we can all enjoy socialising and sharing a hug with our friends and families again!'

Henrietta stretches,
Gives a wiggle, a shake, and a shrug,
And ends her journey,
With Mummy's big hug!

It had been a long and tiring day, so after Henrietta had eaten her tea and hugged her mum one more time, she curled up and snuggled into her bed for a well-earned nap, ready for her next adventure.

Stay safe ...

Lightning Source UK Ltd.
Milton Keynes UK
UKHW051151131121
393861UK00002B/54